THE MESSY MONSTER

Written by Michael J. Pellowski
Illustrated by Diane Paterson

Troll Associates

Library of Congress Cataloging in Publication Data

Pellowski, Michael.
  The messy monster.

  Summary: Sam Skunk and his animal friends, after
having a picnic at the lake, return to find a mess so big
it could only have been made by a monster.
  [1. Litter (Trash)—Fiction. 2. Picnicking—Fiction.
3. Skunks—Fiction. 4. Animals—Fiction] I. Paterson,
Diane, 1946-   ill. II. Title.
PZ7.P3656Me   1986   [E]   85-14064
ISBN 0-8167-0570-4 (lib. bdg.)
ISBN 0-8167-0571-2 (pbk.)

10   9   8   7   6   5   4   3   2

THE MESSY MONSTER

4

Picnics are fun. Do you like picnics? Sam Skunk and his friends liked picnics. They had a good picnic place.

The picnic place had big trees.
It had nice grass. It was by a
lake. What a good place to
picnic! Sam Skunk liked it there.
In the shade of the trees he liked
to sit, eating apples.

Mandy Mouse liked the picnic
place, too. She liked the nice
grass. Mandy liked to sit on the
grass and eat popcorn.

Brown Bear liked the big trees.
He sat by the trees and ate
honey. Bears like to picnic on
honey.

8

Sue Squirrel liked to sit in the
tree tops. She sat and read the
newspaper. She ate nuts.
"What a good picnic place," Sue
said.

Bob Bunny liked the lake. It was a good place to picnic. Bob had carrots and carrot juice by the lake.

"Picnicking is fun!" said Sam
Skunk one day. "I will go on a
picnic."
Sam went to the picnic place.
"Oh no!" said Sam.
What did Sam see? The picnic
place was not nice. It was all
messy!

The mess was not little. It was a big, monstrous mess! It was messy by the trees. The grass was messy. It was messy by the lake.

12

What a mess! There were nutshells, apple cores, and carrot tops. There were newspapers, paper bags, and boxes. Cans were here. Jars were there. And popcorn was everywhere!

13

"Look at this!" yelled Sam.
"What a mess! Who would
make such a mess?"

Sam thought about the mess. He thought and thought. What about his friends? No. Sam had good friends. They would not do such a thing!

15

"There is too much mess," thought Sam. "A mouse could not make it. A squirrel or bunny could not make it. Even a bear is not big enough to make so much mess."
But someone made the mess.

Who? Who was big enough to make a monstrous mess? "What a mystery," said Sam. "I must find out who made this mess. I must solve this messy mystery."

Sam went to see Mandy Mouse.
He told her about the mystery.
He told her about the mess.

"Nutshells and carrot tops?"
said Mandy. "Newspapers,
apple cores, paper bags, and
boxes? Cans and jars and
popcorn? What monster messed
up our picnic place?"

19

"A monster!" cried Sam Skunk.
"A messy monster!" said Mandy
Mouse.
"That's it," said Sam. "A
monster is big enough to make
all that mess."

Mandy looked at her friend. "What does the monster look like?" she asked. "I was at the picnic place. I ate a box of popcorn. I did not see a monster."

Sam thought about the monster.
"I do not know what it looks
like," he said. "I only know I
must find it. I must make it
clean up the picnic place."

Mandy looked at her friend. "What does the monster look like?" she asked. "I was at the picnic place. I ate a box of popcorn. I did not see a monster."

Sam thought about the monster.
"I do not know what it looks
like," he said. "I only know I
must find it. I must make it
clean up the picnic place."

Mandy said, "I want a clean
picnic place, too. I will help you
find the monster. I will help
solve this mystery."
Away went the mouse and the
skunk. They went to see Brown
Bear. They told him about the
monster.

"Did you see a monster?"
Mandy asked.
"It is a big and messy monster,"
said Sam. "It made a monstrous
mess."

24

Brown Bear thought and thought.
"I was at the picnic place," he
said. "I was by the tree. I had
some honey in jars. But I did
not see a monster."

"Where did the monster go?"
asked Mandy. "Someone must
have seen it."
"We must find the monster,"
said Brown Bear. "It must clean
up the mess."

26

Sam did not say anything. He
was thinking. Sam was thinking
about popcorn and popcorn
boxes. He was thinking about
honey jars and apple cores.
Did Sam know something?

"Let's tell Sue Squirrel," said
Mandy. "Maybe she saw the
monster."
Away went the mouse, the bear,
and the skunk.

"A monster?" said Sue Squirrel.
"I did not see it. I went on a
picnic. I sat in a tree top and
read my newspaper. I ate nuts.
But I did not see a monster."

"What a mystery!" said Mandy.
"Where is that monster?" asked
Brown Bear.
"Who will clean the picnic
place?" said Sue.
Sam did not say anything. He
thought and thought.

Away went the friends. Away
they went to solve the mystery.
They went to see Bob Bunny.
"We are looking for a monster,"
said Brown Bear.
"It messed up our nice picnic
place," said Mandy.

Sam Skunk looked at Bob Bunny. "The mess was very big," said Sam. "It was messy by the trees. The grass was messy. It was messy by the lake, too."

Sam went on.

"There were nutshells and carrot tops. There were newspapers, paper bags, apple cores, and boxes. Cans were here. Jars were there. Popcorn was everywhere!"

33

Bob Bunny looked at his friends.
"I picnicked by the lake," he
said. "I had a bag of carrots.
I had carrot juice in a can. But I
did not see a monster."

"No monster?" asked the bear.
"That's funny," said the mouse.
"Where is that monster?" asked
the squirrel.

"I do not know," said Bob
Bunny. "But we must find it.
I like a nice picnic place. I want
that mess cleaned up."

Sam Skunk was thinking.
"Apple cores and nutshells?" he
thought. "Carrots and carrot
tops? Newspapers, bags, and
boxes? Cans and jars?"

Sam looked at his friends.
"And popcorn!" he yelled.
"What?" asked the others.
"The mystery is solved!" Sam
yelled.

"It is?" said Mandy.
"Where is the monster?" asked
Sue.
"What does it look like?" yelled
Brown Bear.
"Popcorn?" said Bob Bunny.

"Let's go to the picnic place,"
said Sam. "There you will see
the messy monster."

Away went the friends. They
went to the picnic place. It was
a mess!

Everyone looked for the
monster. Brown Bear and Bob
Bunny looked. Mandy Mouse
and Sue Squirrel looked. They
looked and looked. Sam Skunk
looked at his friends.

"The monster is here," Sam
said. "It looks like a bear and a
mouse. It looks like a squirrel
and a bunny and a skunk.
Together we are the monster."

43

"What?" yelled Sue.

"Us!" said Bob.

"How?" asked Mandy.

"We all picnicked," said Sam.
"But no one cleaned up. We
each made a little mess.
Together we made a monstrous
mess!"

"That's my popcorn and box,"
said Mandy.
"I see my newspaper and
nutshells," said Sue.
"Those are my honey jars," said
Brown Bear.
"I see my carrot tops, bags, and
juice cans," said Bob.

"And those are my apple cores!" said Sam. "Together we made the mess. Together we can clean it up. We can make our picnic place nice again."

"I'll clean the grass," said Mandy.
"We'll clean by the trees," yelled
Sue and Brown Bear.
"I'll clean by the lake," said Bob.
"Me, too," said Sam Skunk.
Soon the picnic place was nice
again.

And the messy monster? It was
never seen again!